THE THREE QUESTIONS

Based on a story by Leo Tolstoy

Written and illustrated by Jon J Muth

SCHOLASTIC PRESS   NEW YORK

LIBRARY OF CONGRESS CATALOGING-IN-PUBLICATION DATA

Muth, Jon J

The three questions / written and illustrated by Jon J Muth.— 1st ed.   p. cm.

"Based on a story by Leo Tolstoy."

Summary: Nikolai asks his animal friends to help him answer three important questions:

"When is the best time to do things?" "Who is the most important one?"

and "What is the right thing to do?"

ISBN 0-439-19996-4

[1. Conduct of life—Fiction. 2. Animals—Fiction.] I. Tolstoy, Leo, graf, 1828-1910. II. Title.

PZ7.M97274 Th 2001   [Fic]—dc21   00-049673

10   9   8   04   05   06

Printed in Malaysia 46   First edition, April 2002

The illustrations in this book were rendered in watercolor.

Jon J Muth's portrait of Leo Tolstoy in the author's note was rendered in oil.

The text was set in 14-point Hiroshige Book.

The display type was set in Hoefler Requiem Fine.

Book design by David Saylor

For Nikolai

There once was a boy named Nikolai who sometimes felt
uncertain about the right way to act. "I want to be a good person," he told his
friends. "But I don't always know the best way to do that."

Nikolai's friends understood and they wanted to help him.

"If only I could find the answers to my three questions," Nikolai continued,
"then I would always know what to do."

Nikolai's friends considered his first question.

Then Sonya, the heron, spoke. "To know the best time to do things, one must plan in advance," she said.

Gogol, the monkey, who had been rooting through some leaves to find something good to eat, said, "You will know when to do things if you watch and pay close attention."

Then Pushkin, the dog, who was just dozing off, rolled over and said, "You can't pay attention to everything yourself. You need a pack to keep watch and help you decide when to do things. For example, Gogol, a coconut is about to fall on your head!"

Nikolai thought for a moment. Then he asked his second question. "Who is the most important one?"

"Those who are closest to heaven," said Sonya, circling up into the sky.

"Those who know how to heal the sick," said Gogol, stroking his bruised noggin.

"Those who make the rules," growled Pushkin.

Nikolai thought some more. Then he asked the third question. "What is the right thing to do?"

"Flying," said Sonya.

"Having fun all the time," laughed Gogol.

"Fighting," barked Pushkin right away.

Then the boy thought for a long while. He loved his friends. He knew they were all trying their best to help him answer his questions. But their answers didn't seem quite right.

Then, an idea came to him. *I know!* he thought. *I will ask Leo, the turtle. He has lived a very long time. Surely he will know the answers I am looking for.*

Nikolai hiked high up into the mountains where the old turtle lived all alone.

When Nikolai arrived, he found Leo digging a garden. The turtle was old, and digging was hard for him.

"I have three questions and I came to ask your help," Nikolai said. "When is the best time to do things? Who is the most important one? What is the right thing to do?"

Leo listened carefully, but he only smiled.

Then he went on with his digging.

"You must be tired," Nikolai said at last. "Let me help you." The turtle gave him his shovel and thanked him.

And because it was easier for a young boy to dig than it was for an old turtle, Nikolai kept on digging until the rows were finished.

But just as he finished, the wind blew wildly
and rain burst from darkened clouds.
 As they moved toward the cottage for shelter,
Nikolai suddenly heard a cry for help.

Running down the path, he found a panda whose leg had been injured by a fallen tree.

Carefully, Nikolai carried her into Leo's house and made a splint for her leg with a stick of bamboo.

The storm raged on, banging at the doors and windows.
The panda woke up.
"Where am I?" she said. "And where is my child?"

The boy ran out of the cottage and down the path. The roar of the storm was deafening. Pushing against the howling wind and drenching rain, he ran farther into the forest. There he found the panda's child, cold and shivering on the ground.

The little panda was wet and scared, but alive. Nikolai carried her inside
and made her warm and dry. Then he laid her in her mother's arms.

Leo smiled when he saw what the boy had done.

The next morning the sun was warm, birds sang, and all was well with the world. The panda's leg was healing nicely, and she thanked Nikolai for saving her and her baby from the storm.

At that moment, Sonya, Gogol, and Pushkin arrived to make sure everyone was all right.

Nikolai felt great peace within himself. He had wonderful friends. And he had saved the panda and her child. But he also felt disappointed. He still had not found the answers to his three questions. So he asked Leo one more time.

The old turtle looked at the boy.
'But your questions have been answered!" he said.
"They have?" asked the boy.

"Yesterday, if you had not stayed to help me dig my garden, you wouldn't have heard the panda's cries for help in the storm. Therefore, the most important time was the time you spent digging the garden. The most important one at that moment was me, and the most important thing to do was to help me with my garden.

"Later, when you found the injured panda, the most important time was the time you spent mending her leg and saving her child. The most important ones were the panda and her baby. And the most important thing to do was to take care of them and make them safe.

"Remember then that there is only one important time, and that time is now. The most important one is always the one you are with. And the most important thing is to do good for the one who is standing at your side. For these, my dear boy, are the answers to what is most important in this world.

"This is why we are here."

Author's Note

Many years ago I found "The Three Questions" mentioned in a book by Thich Nhat Hanh, a Vietnamese Zen Master. When I first read the story it was as if a golden bell inside me had been struck, reminding me that I already knew this tale by heart. Some books are like that and it has happened for me very often with the writer Leo Tolstoy.

The original short story is not about a boy with animal friends but a Tsar who is looking for answers to "the three questions." His adventure was of a different kind. Rather than saving a panda and her child, he unwittingly rescues someone who is trying to harm him. By saving his enemy, he creates a profound connection with another human being. I encourage those readers interested in sophisticated layers and intrigue to seek out Leo Tolstoy's wonderful original story of the same name.

I wanted to tell this story to a young audience so its form here is somewhat different than Tolstoy's. I hope he would be honored by this telling. I hope it would make him smile.

The animal characters borrow their names from many places. Pushkin and Gogol are the names of famous Russian writers. Sonya was the name of Leo Tolstoy's wife. Nikolai is the name of Leo Tolstoy's brother and also my son, who modeled for the character. Pushkin was modeled for by my dog, Raymond. My daughter Adelaine is the baby panda. And the wise character of Leo is, of course, Tolstoy.

Count Leo Tolstoy (1828–1910) was one of Russia's greatest novelists and one of its most influential moral philosophers and social reformers. He is renowned as the author of *War and Peace* (1865–1869) and *Anna Karenina* (1875–1877), and also as an outstanding thinker of the nineteenth century. His short story, "The Three Questions," on which this book is based, was published in 1903.